To
Genevieve
+
Isabella—

Sadie says

"Think About what you

CAN DO

and not what you

CAN'T DO—

just like me"

Love :

Sadie

Sadie and the Superstars

Aknowledgements:

Thank you to Gary Richter who stepped up and filled in the shoes of his son, Collin, to continue Matt and Dexter's journeys and bring Sadie to life in books, just like she is in real life. Sadie is a real dog who lives in the Midwest with her mom, Joal. Thank you, Gary, for giving millions of hours to this project, despite all the other projects you have going on. Thank you to Paula Goodnight for editing my book with love. Thank you, Joal Derse Dauer, for trusting Sadie's story with me.
It has been a pleasure working on this project with you!
–Allison

Thank you, Allison and Gary for believing in the Power of Sadie. It is with this book, along with the others in the series, that we may teach acceptance of animals and people who have special needs. A very special thank you goes to Doctor Jodie who thought that we should give Sadie a chance.
–Joal

For permission requests, write to the publisher, as follows:
"Attention: Permissions Coordinator"
Allison Schley c/o 2ForeverFriends
2822 St. Andrews Ct.
Waukesha, WI 53188

Printed in the United States of America. First Printing, 2014
ISBN-13:978-1505425451   ISBN-10 15054245X
2ForeverFriends Publishing

Ordering information:
To order, go to www.2ForeverFriends.com
Special discounts are available on quantity purchases.
Book signings and author talks also available.
For details, contact Allison Schley at allison@2ForeverFriends.com.

Sadie and the Superstars

by Allison Schley
and Joal Derse Dauer

Illustrated by
Gary Richter

www.savingsadie.com

Yellow sun shone through the bedroom window.
A small breeze blew the curtains softly.
Matt looked out the window.
"Come on," signed Matt. "Let's go play."

Matt got Dexter's leash.
Dexter knew they were going out to play.
Dexter wagged his tail.
Dexter was a happy dog.

Matt put Dexter's leash on and took him outside.
They ran to the park.
"Time for FUN!" signed Matt, looking around the park.
Dexter lay on the grass and wiggled all over.
Dexter was a silly dog.

"fun"

A blond boy waved to Matt.
Matt waved back and smiled.
"Hi, Matt," signed Zach, walking over to Matt and Dexter.
"Want to play baseball?" signed Zach.

Zach showed Matt his new blue bat.
"I can't wait to use this!" Zach signed.
The boys and Dexter walked over to the baseball diamond.
Boys and girls were all walking towards the field.
The captains, Bob and Sue, took turns picking kids to be on their teams.

Zach heard them call, "Matt!" and signed to Matt that he got picked.
Matt didn't hear his name. He was deaf.
Matt and Zach got put on the same team.
The boys high-fived as they walked across the field to join their team.

"Who is that?" signed Matt, looking across the field at a girl and a dog in a yellow wagon.

"Never saw her before," said John.

Matt looked at Zach. "Do you want me to sign for you?" he asked.

"Yes, please," signed Matt.

Zach signed for Matt when the kids talked so he would know what was going on.
Zach spoke for Matt when he signed so the kids would understand Matt.
"She's new here," said Sue. "She does not talk much."
"Who has a dog in a wagon?" said John. "That's just odd."

Sue walked over to the girl to ask if she wanted to play.

Zach and Matt saw the girl shake her head, "No," and pet her dog.

Sue walked back to the boys and said, "Well, I tried to ask her."

"Maybe later," signed Matt. "Let's play ball!"

CRACK went the bat.
YAY went his team.
The baseball flew into the air,
whirling like a snowball in flight.

John ran to first plate and was safe.
Matt was up to bat next.
CRACK went the bat.
Matt ran and ran.
He didn't stop until he got to home plate.

"WAY TO GO!" screamed the kids.
"WOOHOO!" cheered the kids.

Dexter and Matt didn't hear them.
Both Dexter and Matt were deaf.

15

Dexter ran over to Matt and licked his face.
Matt pet Dexter and smiled.
Dexter always knew when Matt did something special.
Dexter was a special dog.

The kids played and ran for a few hours.
They ran, they laughed, they hit, and they cheered.
Midday, some kids started to leave.
"Have to clean my room," one boy said as he left.
"Have to go to the dentist," another said.

Matt told Zach they should go meet the girl.
"She looks lonely," Matt signed.
"I think Dexter needs a new friend," signed Zach, looking at the dog in the wagon.
The boys and Dexter walked over to the girl and her dog.

"Hi, my name is Zach."
"Hi," said the girl. "My name is Joal."
"I'm Matt," signed Matt.
Zach voiced for Joal so she would understand. "This is Dexter," signed Matt, pointing to Dexter.

"This is Sadie," said the girl.
"Why is Sadie in a wagon?" asked Zach.
"Sadie can't walk," said Joal.
Zach signed for Matt so he knew what she was saying.

Some kids nearby started to point and laugh.
"What kind of dog can't walk?"
Some kids walked away.
None of the kids wanted to play with Sadie.

"Those kids are mean," signed Matt. "No one wanted to play with me or Dexter, because we are deaf. That hurts."
"Some kids are not nice," signed Zach, "Just because the dog can't walk does not mean she is not good."

"Why can't she walk?" signed Matt.
Sadie's owner took a deep breath.
"It is a sad story," she answered. "Sadie was hurt by some bad people. They left her out in the mountains."
Matt and Zach's eyes showed how upset they were.

"Some caring people found her and brought her to Wisconsin. My mom saw Sadie at an animal shelter. My mom fell in love and wanted to help Sadie," the girl added.

The girl gave Sadie a treat. Sadie howled with joy. She was a happy dog.

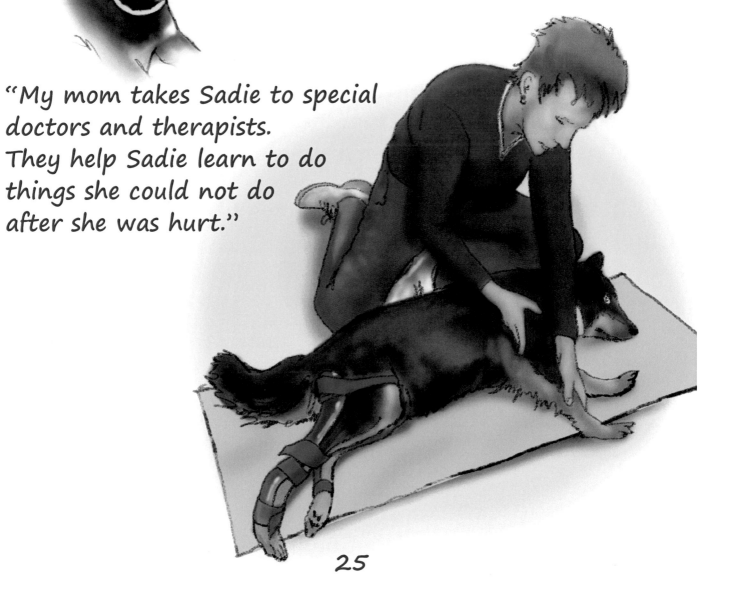

"My mom takes Sadie to special doctors and therapists. They help Sadie learn to do things she could not do after she was hurt."

"That is sad, but also happy!" Matt signed.
Dexter wagged his tail at Sadie.
Sadie wagged her tail back.
Dexter jumped into the wagon, too!

"happy"

26

Dexter sniffed Sadie.
Sadie sniffed Dexter.
Dexter wagged his tail and jumped
around the wagon joyfully.
Dexter knew that even though Sadie could
not walk, she was still a happy dog.

"We are going to ride bikes later,
do you want to come?" asked Matt.
"No," said Joal, shaking her head and looking at Sadie.
"I can't pull Sadie's wagon and ride a bike."
"We could go swimming," suggested Zach.
"Does she like that?"
Joal's eyes lit up. "Yes, Sadie loves to swim!"

The kids agreed to meet at the lake in an hour.
They raced home to get their suits and towels.
Joal was happy the boys wanted to play.
Sadie was happy that Dexter wanted to play.

The kids got to the lake at the same time.
Matt jumped in.
Zach jumped in.
Dexter jumped in.
SPLASH!

Joal carried Sadie out of the wagon.
She gently put Sadie in the water.
Dexter was so happy he splashed the kids and Sadie.

When they were done, the kids and Dexter
got out of the lake.
SHAKY SHAKY SHAKY went Dexter.
Sadie slowly wiggled herself out of the lake.
SHAKY SHAKY SHAKY went Sadie.

Joal scooped Sadie into her wagon.
Sadie loved her wagon.
Sadie could not walk, but in her wagon, she could
go anywhere any other dog could go.

The children decided to get an ice cream cone on the way home.

Matt and Zach marched down the street in front of Joal, who was pulling Sadie in the wagon. Dexter walked proudly next to the wagon and his new friend.

Matt turned and looked at their group. "We look like a parade!" he signed.

The kids laughed and waved at all the
people as they went by.
Adults smiled back. Kids waved back.
"Hey!" said a girl in a wheelchair.
"That dog is just like me."

"What?" asked her mom.
"I have wheels, and she has
wheels," explained the little
girl.

The girl and her mom went over to see Sadie and her friends.

"Can we pet your dog?" the girl asked. "She is like me." "Sure," replied Joal. "Sadie loves to be pet." The girl pet Sadie, and Sadie's tail went WAG WAG WAG.

Ten other kids in wheelchairs wheeled by and stopped to see Sadie.

"We are going to play basketball at the Community Center," said one boy's mom.

"Basketball?" asked Zach, confused. "You can't do that. You are in wheelchairs!"

The mom smiled and one of the girls said, "We might not be able to run, but we play some pretty good basketball! Come and watch."

The kids and dogs went into the Community Center to see what the girl was talking about. The kids all rolled onto the court and each of them grabbed a ball.

Music started blasting, telling them practice time was starting. The boys and girls wheeled their chairs in circles and passed the balls to each other.

"Wow," signed Matt. "They play better than I do!"

The kids took turns shooting hoops.

Sadie wagged her tail and howled.
Dexter wagged his tail and barked.
Matt, Zach and Joal cheered.
The kids smiled.

Matt looked at Dexter and Sadie.
Zach looked at the kids in wheelchairs.
"We all have special needs," he said,
"But we all have special abilities, too!"

"She's just like us!" screamed the kids in wheelchairs, watching Sadie ride in her wagon.
"She should be our mascot."
"Yeah!" said the parents. "Let's call our team 'Sadie's Superstars!'"

The children all loved Sadie. Matt, Zach, and Joal all said, "Goodbye!" to the other kids.
They marched off down the road, with Joal pulling Sadie in her yellow wagon.

The kids were so excited as they wheeled down the street and cheered, "Go, Sadie, go! If she can, we can!"

Made in the USA
San Bernardino, CA
14 April 2015

SADIE AND THE SUPERSTARS

Life can be difficult when you are looked at as "different" and not accepted. Meet Sadie, the real dog that no one wanted. She teaches us to focus on what you CAN DO and not what you CAN'T DO. Sadie lives with Joal and they travel extensively teaching acceptance and instructing others how to stop the cycle of abuse. This inspirational story will warm your heart! You just may think of adopting a shelter dog with special needs, just like Sadie!

ABOUT THE AUTHORS

Allison Schley is the author of the Forever Friends' series. Allison lives in Wisconsin with her husband, Bill, two children, Megan and Zach, three cats and a dog named Carlton.

Allison grew up in Ohio and attended Beachwood Schools. It is there she learned to use sign language and befriended children with hearing loss. These friendships led her on a journey and to a lifelong passion to work with children with hearing loss. She has been in the field of Deaf Education for 20 years and founded Communication Connections, Inc., a nonprofit dedicated to early intervention for families with hearing loss. When she isn't working, Allison can be found enjoying time with her family, selling 3 D Mascara, and taking walks with Carlton.

Joal Derse Dauer was raised in suburban Milwaukee, and has had a passion for animals since early childhood. She uses this passion as an animal activist, teacher, lecturer and author to share Sadie's story. Through her story, she hopes to promote acceptance of people and animals with special needs and to stop the cycle of animal abuse.

ABOUT THE ILLUSTRATOR

Gary Richter is the father of Collin Richter, the original illustrator of Allison's two previous books. Gary has continued the characters as Collin would have, had he not moved away to college this year. Collin had come to understand some of the challenges of hearing loss through his older sister, Becca Richter, a singer/songwriter who has a partial hearing loss since birth.

ISBN 9781505425451

9 781505 425451

9000

Cowboy Welles

Lauren Seiler and Pam Duke